Keith G Davis

OXALIS

A Story of Renewal

BY KEITH GADDY DAVIS

OXALIS *A Story of Renewal*

ISBN 0-9647751-2-3

CLAYTON PAIGE PUBLISHING COMPANY
TOLL FREE 1-888-585-8909
P.O. BOX 581032
MINNEAPOLIS, MN 55458-1032

Book Design: PEGGY LAURITSEN DESIGN GROUP, MINNEAPOLIS   *Photography:* JOHN HAINES

She was in one of those twenty-four hour a day coffee shops. You know the kind; three booths at the window, nine stools at the counter. They are famous for breakfast and talk. The chalkboard menu features homemade cinnamon rolls, hash browns, eggs any way you want them and a bottomless cup of non-designer coffee. By virtue of their size these places bring people together.

Except for the woman in a booth by the window, an unseen cook and an overtired waitress, the place was empty. It was after three in the morning. I ordered coffee and sat at the counter. From where I was seated, I could see her looking out the window in which she was reflected. Tears periodically welled up in her eyes and spilled down her cheeks. She wiped them away with a crumpled tissue held in her left hand. From time to time a single tear would make it all the way down her face. She stared out the window ignoring the coffee, long since gone cold in her cup.

"Is there something I can do?" I offered. "I'd like to help."

I felt awkward in the silence that grew around my question. A few long moments later the words found her. She slowly turned her head toward me. The eyes that met mine were filled with concentrated sadness. Her words, preceded by a long exhale with which her shoulders sank, were flat and measured, without energy.

"No, no thank you. There's nothing anyone can do for me."

After a moment she whispered, "Excuse me." She gathered her things and left.

A clinician would have charted; "Depressed affect."

Having been intimately acquainted with depression, I wanted to break into her pain with some offer of help. Sadness settled around me as I watched her disappear into the darkness.

I took my coffee, sat down in the booth she had vacated and stared out the window. Raindrops, in what appeared to be random patterns, slid down the pane and collected in pools on the sill.

I sipped my coffee and remembered another time, a time of multiplied misery in my life when I struggled with depression. During that terrible time, all the foolishness, all the mistakes and all the failures of my life seemed to concentrate in one overwhelming event.

The ideas I had of myself, my expectations of life and my beliefs about how I fit into the overall scheme of things were shattered.

I felt guilt and shame. In fact, shame became the medium in which I existed. I could neither face myself nor others. Over time, I moved down past depression. Despair, creating a barrier between me and the rest of the world, shrouded my days. Most nights were sleepless. When sleep did come, it was intermittent and unrefreshing. I felt exhausted, isolated . . . hopeless.

I withdrew and closed the doors of my life on any offers of help with the exact same words she said to me.

"No, no thank you. There's nothing any one can do for me."

I stayed alive yet ceased to live.

During the early spring of one of those dreadful years, a friend gave me a plant in a simple clay pot. She thrust the gift into my misery as she cheerfully said, "I know things have been difficult for you for a long time. This is a happy springtime oxalis plant. You'll love it. It's filled with wonder."

She was gone before I could object.

I did not want to be responsible for any living thing. I resented her cheerful investment
in life. More than that, I resented the way she turned words around, attempting to
squeeze the meaning out of them and into me.

"Filled with wonder."

"Wonderful. The word is wonderful." I wanted to shout after her.

It is almost impossible for people who are not depressed to know how we feel. We almost, sort of, look OK. They seem to think if only we would snap out of it, cheer up, or just *do* something, we would feel better.

"Well it isn't that easy, plant lady!"

I promptly forgot the name of the plant, put it on top of a bookcase, where it sat, eventually supporting the ends of cobwebs before it drooped, turned brown and died. From time to time, when I glanced up at it, the plant would add a new dimension to my guilt. It was a visual reminder of neglect, an additional failure.

The following spring, while walking past a local flower shop, I noticed a huge display of the same kind of plant my friend had given me. The display, being built by an energetic worker, nearly filled the window. The plants were lush and green with delicate, white, trumpet-like flowers supported on slender stems. I walked into the shop for a closer look.

A pang of guilt about my own plant was interrupted by the words, "May I help you?"

Something inside me moved. Time seemed to slow as I struggled with my usual response of, "No, no thank you, there's nothing anyone can do for me." Deliberately, I made the decision to say . . . "Yes."

"Yes. Can you tell me what kind of plant that is?"

"Sure," She said, "It's oxalis. It's really wonderful."

"Yeah, I have one." After a pause, I added, "It died."

She started adding more plants to the display. Without stopping she asked,
"Do you still have it?"

"Yes, I still have it."

"Then it's probably not dead forever."

"It died a long time ago," I said, emphasizing long.

"Cut off the dead foliage, soak it in water, set it in a sunny window. It'll come back
to life." She continued building the display as matter of factly as she had spoken.
Absorbed in her work, she never looked at me again.

Several days later, I cleared the cobwebs and brought my plant down from the dusty shelf. Dry stems broke away at a touch. I took a pair of scissors and cut back what was left of the foliage, making it even with the top of the hard-packed soil. As I was doing this, I remembered reading articles about plants having intelligence and feelings. I wondered about the sensation of the severe pruning. Stupid thought. It's a plant. It's dead. It feels nothing.

I had no qualms about submerging it, pot and all, in water. After it was soaked, I set it in a sunny east-facing window.

Nothing happened.

Then, so slowly as to be almost imperceptible, it changed. Small bumps appeared as some mysterious force pushed stems out of the depths, up through the soil and into space. It grew. The stems set leaves. Some stems bore flowers. It flourished.

I wondered again about the pruning, soaking, and sunlight the plant endured.

I was so sure that it was dead yet there it was vibrantly alive.

I know some things about plant life from science classes: water, sunshine, soil and time. Still there is more to life than can be explained by science. The facts of science do not explain mystery, and something mysterious happened in that clay pot. Call it what you will—renewal, restoration, resurrection. There was life again. Life that as the poet says, "Enjoys the air it breathes."

As I watched that plant come to life, a part of the tangled depression inside me opened. It was clear that I, like my oxalis plant, needed help to live. If life could be renewed in that clay pot, maybe, just maybe life could be healthy, whole, healed up again for me.

Something inside me strained toward life.

I became a gardener.

The tiny seeds I hold in my hand each year have no discernible signs of life. I press them into the earth and wait: water, sunshine, time and mystery.

Something beyond understanding happens. Life begins. The seeds become plants.

My experience with the oxalis plant and gardening taught me some lessons. With help I was able to bring those lessons into my life. There were parts of my self-centered despair that needed to be pruned. The accumulated habits of depression had to undergo more than one cleansing before they began to untangle. Allowing light into the isolated darkness I had kept so well tended was a slow, painful process. The light was so revealing at times that I needed additional help to steady myself.

The most important lesson I learned is that in this world there is a mystery that wills vital, vigorous, vibrant life with such power that even death is not the end.

Only in retrospect am I aware of the chain of events that contributed to my growth.

It began when my friend thrust the oxalis plant into my depression. It continued when the woman in the flower shop asked if she could help. The critical moment came when I made the deliberate decision to accept help.

No one could have noticed it, but that was the moment when my depression broke open and growth began. Slowly, imperceptibly, mysteriously despair began to dissipate. Depression dissolved and finally disappeared.

Now when I glance at my oxalis plant I feel no pangs of guilt or shame. It no longer reminds me of neglect and failure. Instead it is a visual reminder of renewal and restoration.

Life for me is healthy, whole and healed up. I am hopeful in any circumstance. I see flowers bloom in the cracks of barren asphalt, violets blossoming in late spring snows and the earth restored each year. I have seen life renewed in a simple clay pot.

The oxalis plant reminds me that this is a resurrection world.

I wanted to talk with the woman in the coffee shop. She left before we had the opportunity. I do not know who she is or where she is. I do not know about the origins of her sadness.

I would like to be the one to give her an oxalis plant and tell her, "It's filled with wonder."

I want her to know there is no difficulty beyond help, no past beyond redemption and nothing beyond forgiveness.

This story is my letter to her. I hope it finds its way into her life. Until it does it will not be complete.

Somehow I feel it's not so much a story about me or a woman in a coffee shop as it is a story about all of us who sometimes need help and sometimes have help to offer.

OXALIS is my way of offering, "Is there something I can do, I'd like to help."

From me to you, the story's yours.

Oxalis is the botanical name for wood sorrel. The oxalis family consists of a group of more than 800 species of small bulbous plants producing delicate pentamerous flowers with trifoliate clover-like leaves. The leaves close up at night. In warm climates it is a tuberous perennial. In northern climates it is most commonly used as a house plant. Oxalis is propagated by bulbs, divisions or by seeds.

Depression: A pathological state of excessive hopelessness characterized by feelings of inadequacy, fatigue, poor concentration, social withdrawal, sadness and sometimes physical symptoms. (Oxford English Dictionary and DSM-IV 1994, published by the American Psychiatric Association, Washington, D.C.)

If you think you are depressed, please seek the help of a physician or counseling professional.
If you would like a discussion guide for OXALIS, call toll free 1-(888)-585-8909